P9-CFU-850

SCIENCE AND ARTS ACADEMY
1825 MINER STREET
DES PLAINES, IL 60016

Kami and the Yaks

Kami and

Andrea Stenn Stryer

Illustrated by Bert Dodson

the Yaks

T 11356

Bay Otter Press

Palo Alto, California

© 2007 Andrea Stenn Stryer

Bay Otter Press is an imprint of

New Spectrum, Inc.

P.O. Box 20492

Palo Alto, California 94309

CATALOGING-IN-PUBLICATION DATA

Stryer, Andrea Stenn.
Kami and the yaks / by Andrea Stenn Stryer ; illustrated by Bert Dodson.
   p.   cm.
   SUMMARY: In the Himalaya Mountains of Nepal, a deaf Sherpa boy
proves himself to his family by rescuing the family's yaks.
Audience: Ages 4–8.
   ISBN 0-9778961-0-2 (cloth)   ISBN 0-9778961-1-0 (pbk.)

   1. Sherpa (Nepalese people)—Himalaya Mountains—Juvenile
fiction. 2. Deaf children—Juvenile fiction. I. Dodson, Bert. II. Title.

   PZ7.S9278KAM   2006
   QBI06-600142

Printed in Hong Kong

Kami and the Yaks was produced by Wilsted & Taylor, with production
management by Christine Taylor, production assistance by Drew Patty,
copy editing by Melody Lacina, design and composition by Tag Savage,
printer's bedevilment by Lillian Marie Wilsted, and color supervision by
Susan Schaefer. Printed through Stacy Quinn, QuinnEssentials, Inc.

*In memory
of Danny B.*

Ḥigh in a land where winds blow snow clouds off tall mountain peaks, Kami stepped out into the early morning dark. He sniffed the moistness.

His father and his older brother earned their living by guiding, setting up camp, and cooking for mountain climbers. Since they were starting a trek at sunrise, they had to load the animals with pots, stove, food, and tents right away.

On the slopes, Kami could see two pine-bough torches that his father and his older brother were carrying to search for their four yaks.

Why didn't the yaks come down by themselves, as they usually do? Kami wondered. He looked up again to where Father and Norgay were searching.

No! That's not where the yaks will be.
They like the meadow near the monk's lodge.
He took from his pocket his prize
possession, a shiny tin whistle that a
climber had given him.

Curly Horn, the largest yak, always came when he heard a whistle. So Kami took a big breath, puffed his cheeks, and blew the whistle.

Its buzz tickled his lips, though he could not hear its shrill call because he was deaf.

Kami began to climb. He crossed a gulley and worked his way up the hillside until he reached the meadow near the monk's lodge.

He blew his whistle again.
In the faint light, he searched the ground.

No yak droppings here.

S uddenly, a fork of lightning flashed
across the dark sky, singeing the air.
Kami smelled the sizzle and wrinkled his nose.
Thunder rumbled. Kami felt it, like
the vibrating drumbeats at temple festivals.
His heart began to race.
I must find the yaks before the storm comes!

He darted to the meadow beyond and
for the third time blew his whistle.
Curly Horn, please be there, he pleaded silently.
But the meadow was empty.

Another bolt of lightning
brightened the sky.
The odor was stronger.
Prickles ran along
Kami's arms. The air
rumbled in answer
to the lightning.

Kami ran toward the thick brush.
No sign of the yaks there, either.
He took great gulps of air.
The lightning flashed again,
looking like skeleton fingers
reaching for him.
He screeched and
clenched his fists.

One more place,
he thought.
I'll try beyond the crags.
He blew his whistle, which made
him feel braver. Scuttling through
the rocks, Kami came to two huge
boulders. As he slipped between
them, he recognized three dark
silhouettes standing and one
lying on the ground.

The yaks. Kami jumped with joy.
He blew his whistle, expecting
Curly Horn to start toward him.
The yak looked at Kami but did
not budge.

Running to Curly Horn, Kami tugged on his thick woven collar. Still, the big yak would not stir. Kami tugged again, then looked around. White Spot, lying down, was pawing at the earth.

Kami dropped Curly Horn's collar and dashed to the littlest yak. He flung his arms around him and pulled.

Get up, please get up, Kami grunted. *Don't be lazy!*

White Spot struggled frantically, then stopped.
Another bolt of lightning shot across the sky.
Kami shivered as the thunder followed.

He saw that the
yak's hind leg was
stuck deep in a
crevice between
two heavy
rocks.

Kami crouched and looked into White Spot's
frightened eyes. He stroked his hairy head.

I'll bring help soon.

He blew his whistle, hoping
to alert Father or Norgay.
But thunder again rumbled,
pulsing the air.

Hail started to fall.

Kami tried to run down the mountain, but the path was now icy with the frozen pebbles.

The hail pelted his face, blurring the way.

He fell, hitting his shoulder on a rock. Rubbing the sore spot, he sniffled. With tears welling up in his eyes, Kami could barely see. He shuffled forward to keep his footing.

He came to the gulley and skidded into it. The other side was now as slippery as yak butter.

Kami tumbled backward.

A streak of lightning lit the river of hail in the gulley.
Kami trembled as the clap of thunder shook the air.
He inched his way on hands and knees. Holding
his breath, he crept slowly. His mittens got wet
and icy. Hail hit his neck and slid down his back.

Little by little, he made it to the gulley's edge.
When he got his knees over the top,
he took a deep breath.

Zigzagging back and forth, Kami finally reached the stone wall that bordered the village path. He rubbed his freezing mittens along the round rocks.

Near the house, he saw Norgay returning. Father was in front of the house, shoulders hunched.

Because he never heard words, Kami was not able to speak. Instead, he grabbed his father's hand and pointed up to the meadow.

Father was angry.

He picked Kami up and plumped him down inside the doorstep.

You don't understand, Kami thought. *I can help. I know where the yaks are!*

Then he took out his whistle and blew three long blasts.

But his father paid no attention.

Kami hopped back over the large step and frantically pulled at Norgay's jacket. He put his mittened hands to his head and imitated the yak's horns.

Norgay stared at his little brother. Kami lowered his head with his hands curved forward and lumbered in a yak-like walk.

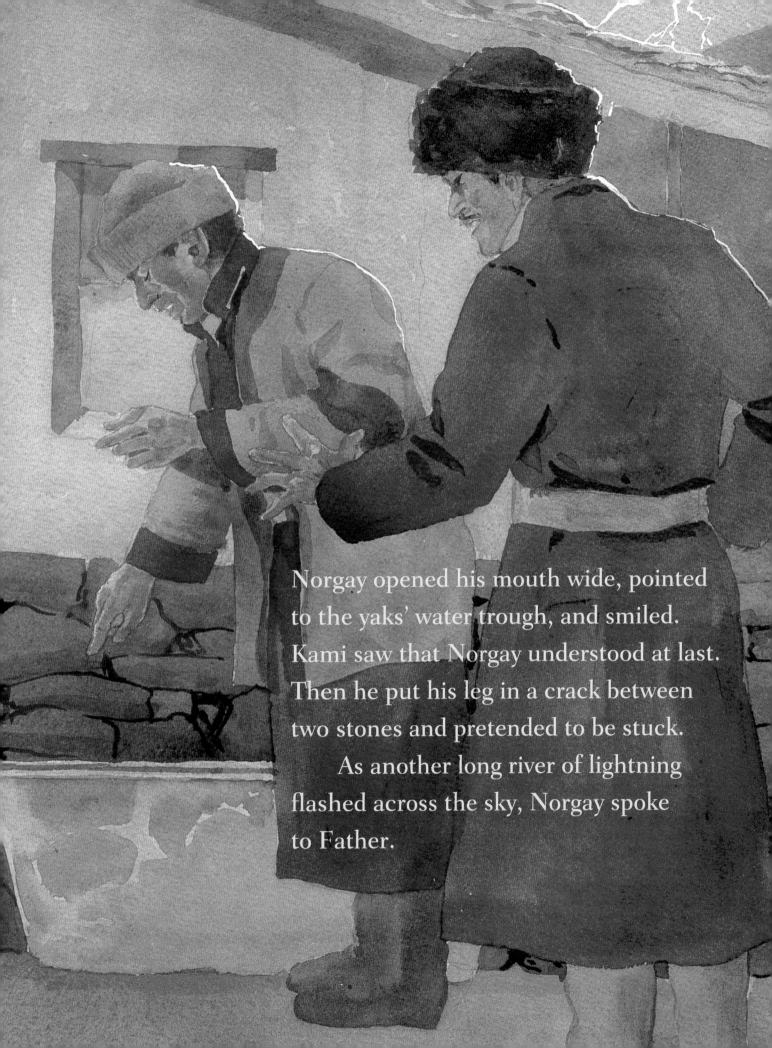

Norgay opened his mouth wide, pointed
to the yaks' water trough, and smiled.
Kami saw that Norgay understood at last.
Then he put his leg in a crack between
two stones and pretended to be stuck.

As another long river of lightning
flashed across the sky, Norgay spoke
to Father.

Father nodded and grabbed a shovel.
He and Norgay followed Kami up, up,
far up the mountain.

Kami led them behind the boulders
and pointed to White Spot.
Father and Norgay ran to the trapped yak.
Together they moved one of the heavy
rocks and freed his hind leg.

White Spot struggled to his feet. Father, brow wrinkled, rubbed his fingers carefully along the leg. He sighed with relief.

Kami ran into Father's arms.
Father picked him up and
clasped him to his chest.

Father put him down in front
of Curly Horn. Kami took the
big yak's thick woven collar in his hand.
Immediately, the other yaks fell in line.
Kami grinned at Father.
I did it, and he knows I did it!

Kami tugged on Curly Horn's collar.

Kami proudly led the yaks, his father, and his brother down the mountain.

Kami and his family are Sherpas, people who first came to the Everest region of Nepal from Tibet some 500 years ago, bringing with them the culture of their eastern neighbor. Their language is a dialect of Tibetan. And they share the Buddhist faith, with its colorful prayer flags, mantra-carved mani-stones, and monasteries throughout the mountainous area.

The Sherpas have great stamina and are accustomed to living at extremely high altitudes. In the very short growing season, they cultivate potatoes, barley, and buckwheat. They also raise yaks, the most useful domestic animals at such heights and in such inclement weather. These shaggy, humped bovines are a crucial part of the Sherpa economy. They provide dairy products, meat, leather, wool, and dung for fuel and fertilizer.

Because the terrain is so rugged, wheels are useless for transportation. Building material, goods to be sold at the market, trekking gear, and even sick people have to be carried on yaks or by the Sherpas themselves.

Since the British first showed interest in conquering the highest peaks almost a century ago, the Sherpas have hired themselves and their yaks to climbers and trekkers. They guide, carry loads, set up camp, cook meals, and watch out for the safety and well-being of climbers. This is how Kami's family earns its livelihood.

Except for summer, when they graze their yaks in the highest pastures, Sherpas live in villages. Their homes are usually two stories high. The lower story, built of stone, houses the animals and provides storage space for food and equipment. A narrow stairway leads to the wooden upper story, which comprises one large room with a stove at one end, a decorated corner for prayers, and a bench along the length of one wall. This bench is where the family sits during the day and sleeps at night. Above the stove are bowls, pans, cups, and plates. Often a loom occupies part of the living space.

Sherpa families are very close-knit. They share both hard work and play. On some evenings after a supper of potato pancakes and yak cheese, Kami's family will tell stories and sing and, with a drum beating, dance.